Every morning, Ben's puppy, Muddypaws, jumped on Ben's bed to wake him up.

And every morning they cuddled before starting the day.

But this morning was different. This morning Ben jumped out of bed and woke Muddypaws with a shout.

"It's Christmas Eve!" yelled Ben.

"What's all the fuss about?" thought Muddypaws.

Ben ran downstairs and Muddypaws followed.

A lot of strange things were happening in the house, and everyone was busy. Muddypaws wanted to be busy, too. Muddypaws wanted to help.

"I need to hang my stocking by the chimney," said Ben.
"And look, there are some more decorations in this box.
Let's make the house as Christmassy as it can be!"

Muddypaws watched as Ben pulled out garlands and
ribbons and ornaments and big silver stars.

Muddypaws saw how he could help. He grabbed a mouthful of decorations between his teeth. He rushed past Ben with a ...

whoosh!

Shake!

Swish!

"Oh, Muddypaws!" Ben laughed. "Maybe I'll do the decorations later."

Ben and Muddypaws went into the kitchen. There were so many wonderful new smells. Muddypaws licked his lips.

"Mom's been making a Christmas cake and cookies,"
said Ben, nibbling at some tasty leftovers.

Muddypaws decided to help clean the floor.

Sniff! Lick!

Then he jumped onto the
chair and inspected the
table. There was a lot
of food to clean
up there, too!

"Not the cookies!" shouted Ben.

He shooed Muddypaws out of the kitchen.

Muddypaws scampered into the living room. Underneath the Christmas tree, he found a pile of presents, all wrapped with pretty paper. Muddypaws sniffed at them, one by one. He smelled soap and clothes and books and slippers. But one smelled very different.

Puppy treats!
Muddypaws knew who
puppy treats were for.

They were a present for him!

He tugged a little with his teeth ...

then a little bit more ...

and more.   Suddenly ...

The treats rolled across the floor, into corners, under chairs, and over all the other presents. Muddypaws suddenly saw how he could be the most helpful puppy of all on this exciting Christmas Eve.
He cleaned up the treats, very, very carefully.

Each and every one.

Muddypaws felt very full and very tired. He rolled himself in the torn wrapping paper until it was wrapped around him like a snug blanket.

When Ben came in, he saw a funny-shaped, snoring present under the tree. "Oh, Muddypaws. You opened your present early!" he said. "But don't worry ... Tomorrow you can help me open mine!"

Merry Christmas, Muddypaws!